Between Two Worlds

Rafik Seddik

Published by Rafik Seddik, 2024.

BETWEEN TWO WORLDS

First edition. August 13, 2024.

ISBN: 979-8227867957

Written by Rafik Seddik.

Title: Between Two Worlds

Chapter 1: A New Beginning

Li Wei stepped off the plane at Heathrow Airport, her heart pounding with a mix of excitement and trepidation. The air was thick with the scent of jet fuel and the murmur of countless languages, a symphony of voices that played a constant background melody. It was a stark reminder that she had indeed arrived in a different world. London this sprawling metropolis she had only known through books and movies was now her reality. The city represented more than just a place; it was a dream, a symbol of freedom, and the gateway to a life she had long envisioned. Here, in this foreign land, she could escape the confining expectations of her traditional upbringing in Guangzhou and embrace the endless possibilities of the West.

As she walked through the terminal, the clattering of trolleys and the rhythmic shuffle of footsteps created a kind of urban music. Li Wei moved like a thread through the fabric of the crowd, weaving her way through throngs of travelers, each with their own story, each a part of the intricate tapestry of the airport. She clutched the handle of her suitcase, her knuckles white against the cold metal, as if holding on to the last vestiges of the life she was leaving behind. Yet, even as she stepped forward, she couldn't shake the sensation that a part of her remained rooted in Guangzhou, tethered by invisible strings to the familiar and the known.

The cool, crisp air of London greeted her as she exited the terminal, a stark contrast to the humid warmth of her hometown. The city's atmosphere was different not just in temperature but in its very essence. The sky was a vast expanse of gray, clouds hanging low like a heavy quilt, as if threatening to engulf the city below. She inhaled deeply, the cold air filling her lungs with a sharpness that was both invigorating and unsettling. The air had a dampness to it, carrying with it the faint scent of rain-soaked earth and the distant aroma of brewing coffee from the airport cafés. She pulled her coat tighter around her slender frame, savoring the unfamiliar sensation of cold air nipping at her cheeks. It was as though the city was embracing her in its own cold, aloof way, and she welcomed the change, the sense of stepping into a new chapter of her life, even if it meant leaving behind everything she had known.

The taxi ride to her student accommodation was a blur of rain-slicked streets, red double-decker buses, and iconic black cabs. The windows were streaked with rain, the droplets chasing each other down the glass, blurring the outside world into a watercolor of gray and red. The buildings loomed over her, their old brick facades soaked in history, and she marveled at the seamless blend of the ancient and the modern. The taxi driver, a man with graying hair and a thick Cockney accent, made small talk as they drove through the city, but his words barely registered. Li Wei was too absorbed in the sights around her. The grandeur of London was overwhelming, the sheer scale of it all daunting. Yet, within the vastness, there was a sense of intimacy—a feeling that each corner, each cobblestone, had a story to tell.

She caught glimpses of landmarks she had only seen in books or on the screen the Tower of London, its ancient stones whispering tales of the past; the Thames, winding its way through the city like a silver ribbon, its surface reflecting the brooding sky above; and the Houses of Parliament, with Big Ben standing tall, a sentinel watching over the capital. These were not just buildings or monuments; they were symbols of a history that stretched back centuries, a history that now, in some small way, she was becoming a part of.

Her accommodation was a modest room in a shared student house in Bloomsbury, not far from the British Museum. The house itself was old, its walls thick with stories of the students who had lived there before her. The bricks were weathered, the mortar between them cracked and uneven, as if time itself had pressed its weight upon the building. The wooden floors creaked underfoot as she made her way up the narrow staircase, the sound echoing through the otherwise silent house. The air was filled with the faint scent of musty books and damp wood, a smell that seemed to belong to another era. As she unpacked her suitcase, the weight of her journey began to settle on her shoulders. The photographs of her family, carefully placed on her desk, seemed to gaze back at her, their faces frozen in time, reminding her of the life she had temporarily left behind. Her mother had been tearful at the airport, clutching her hand and reminding her to eat well and study hard. Her father, though more composed, had a stern yet loving look in his eyes, as if to say, "Make us proud."

Her fiancé, Zhang Yufei, had been supportive of her decision to study abroad, yet his presence loomed large in her thoughts. Their families had arranged their engagement, a union meant to strengthen business ties between their fathers' companies. Yufei was kind, reliable, and everything her family desired for her. But was he what she wanted? Their last conversation before her departure had been a mixture of encouragement and underlying tension. Yufei had urged her to seize the opportunity, but she could see the flicker of uncertainty in his eyes, a shadow of doubt that mirrored her own. It was as though they both understood, without saying it, that this journey was not just about her education it was about discovering who she truly was, and perhaps, who she wanted to become.

As she settled into her new life at the University of London, Li Wei found solace in her studies. Her days were filled with lectures, library sessions, and the occasional sightseeing adventure with her new friends. The university's campus was a blend of historic buildings and modern facilities, a testament to its long-standing academic excellence. The grand old structures stood like sentinels of knowledge, their stone walls and ivy-covered facades exuding a sense of timelessness, while the newer buildings, with their sleek lines and modern architecture, represented the institution's forward-thinking spirit.

She marveled at the grandeur of the Senate House Library, its vast collection of books and manuscripts providing a treasure trove of knowledge. The library itself was a place of reverence, the silence within its walls almost tangible, broken only by the soft rustle of pages turning and the occasional cough. The high ceilings, adorned with intricate moldings, and the rows upon rows of bookshelves filled her with a sense of awe. Here, she could lose herself in the words of the greats, and perhaps, find a way to understand her own story. The scent of old paper and leather-bound volumes was intoxicating, a smell that carried the weight of history, of minds that had pondered the very questions she now grappled with.

Her fellow students were a diverse group, hailing from all corners of the globe. There was Amara from Nigeria, whose infectious laughter and boundless energy made her an instant friend. Amara was a whirlwind of enthusiasm, her presence a bright spot in the often gray London days. She had a way of making even the most mundane activities feel like an adventure, and her stories of life in Lagos were as vivid as the colorful prints she wore. Emily from Australia, with her easygoing demeanor and love for adventure, quickly became her travel buddy. Emily was a free spirit, her love for the outdoors and penchant for spontaneous road trips a stark contrast to Li Wei's more reserved nature. And then there was Rajesh from India, whose sharp intellect and thoughtful insights made him a valuable study partner. Rajesh was quiet, almost reserved, but when he spoke, his words carried weight. His knowledge of literature was vast, and their discussions often stretched late into the night, each pushing the other to think more deeply, more critically.

Despite the initial culture shock, Li Wei embraced the challenges of living in a foreign country. She learned to navigate the intricate web of the London Underground, its maze of tunnels and platforms a world unto itself. The rhythmic clatter of the trains, the rush of air as they approached, and the blur of faces passing by became familiar, comforting in their own way. She found her favorite local café, a small, tucked-away place where she could sip on a cup of Earl Grey while reading, the steam from the tea mingling with the aroma of freshly baked scones. The café became her sanctuary, a place where she could momentarily escape the pressures of her new life and lose herself in the words of Austen, Brontë, and Woolf. The café's walls were lined with shelves of books, their spines worn and faded, each one a potential companion for her solitary afternoons.

She even began to appreciate the unpredictable weather, finding a strange comfort in the ever-present clouds and the way the rain seemed to cleanse the city, leaving the air fresh and cool. There was a rhythm to the weather, a kind of poetry in the way the rain would begin as a soft drizzle, almost imperceptible, before turning into a downpour that rattled against the windows. And then, just as suddenly, it would stop, leaving behind a world that glistened with the promise of renewal.

Her English improved rapidly, though she still found herself stumbling over idiomatic expressions and cultural references. It was in these moments, when she struggled to find the right words, that the distance between her old life and her new one seemed most pronounced. Yet, with each misstep, she grew more confident, her language skills a bridge between her past and her future. She became adept at reading between the lines, understanding the nuances of a language that was not her own, but was quickly becoming a part of her.

One evening, as she was returning from the library, her arms laden with books, she found herself caught in a sudden downpour. The rain was relentless, soaking through her clothes and plastering her hair to her head. She ducked into the nearest building for shelter, only to find herself in a small, dimly lit art gallery. The walls were adorned with paintings, their colors vibrant against the muted light. The air was thick with the scent of oil paint and varnish, a smell that reminded her of the art classes she had taken as a child. She wandered through the gallery, her wet shoes squeaking against the polished floor, the rain forgotten as she lost herself in the art around her.

It was here that she met Edward, a fellow student and art enthusiast. He was standing in front of a large canvas, his head tilted slightly as he studied the brushstrokes with a critical eye. Edward was tall, with unruly brown hair that fell into his eyes, and a demeanor that was both relaxed and intense. His clothes were rumpled, as if he had dressed in a hurry, and his fingers were stained with ink, a sign of his artistic pursuits. He turned to her as she approached, a smile playing on his lips as if he had been expecting her.

"You're soaked," he said with a chuckle, his accent a melodious mix of British and something else she couldn't quite place. There was warmth in his voice, a kind of easy charm that immediately put her at ease.

She smiled, brushing a strand of wet hair from her face. "It's London, I suppose," she replied, her own accent still carrying the soft lilt of Cantonese. There was something about him, a kind of magnetic pull that made her want to stay and talk, to learn more about this stranger who seemed so at ease in a world she was still navigating.

They struck up a conversation, initially about the art that surrounded them—the bold strokes of color, the subtle interplay of light and shadow, the way each piece seemed to tell its own story. Edward spoke passionately about his favorite artists, his words flowing like a river, full of energy and insight. He had a way of making the art come alive, of making her see it not just as images on a canvas, but as expressions of the soul. He was an artist himself, he explained, though he modestly downplayed his talents.

As the conversation deepened, they talked of more than just art. They spoke of life in London, of the challenges and joys of living in a city that was both welcoming and overwhelming. Edward had been born in England, but his mother was French, and he had spent much of his childhood moving between the two countries. His perspective on the world was shaped by this duality, by the blending of cultures that had become a part of who he was.

Li Wei found herself captivated by Edward's stories, by the way he spoke of the world with such passion and curiosity. He was unlike anyone she had ever met free-spirited, creative, and unafraid to challenge the status quo. In him, she saw a reflection of the life she longed to lead, a life unbound by the expectations of others.

Yet, even as she felt herself drawn to Edward, a part of her held back, the weight of her engagement to Zhang Yufei pressing down on her like a heavy cloak. The memory of their last conversation lingered in her mind, a reminder of the life she had left behind in Guangzhou. Yufei was everything her family wanted for her stable, reliable, and deeply rooted in their shared culture. But in the presence of Edward, she couldn't help but question whether stability and reliability were enough.

As they stood in the gallery, the rain still pounding against the windows, Li Wei felt a strange sense of contentment. She was in a foreign city, far from home, surrounded by strangers and uncertainties, and yet, for the first time in a long while, she felt a spark of something new—something that had been missing in her life. Was it the thrill of the unknown? The allure of possibility? Or was it simply the joy of being herself, free from the expectations that had always defined her?

As the evening wore on, the conversation between Li Wei and Edward meandered through various topics, each one revealing more about their personalities and the lives they had led up to this point. Edward spoke of his travels through Europe, his love for the art of the Renaissance, and his belief that life was meant to be lived passionately and fully. He was studying fine arts at the university, but his true love was painting—an expression of his innermost thoughts and emotions. He showed her a sketchbook he carried with him, its pages filled with quick, expressive drawings that captured moments of beauty and emotion in a way words could not.

Li Wei found herself sharing more than she had intended about her life in Guangzhou, her family's expectations, and the burden of an engagement she hadn't truly chosen. Edward listened with a quiet intensity, his gaze never leaving her face as she spoke, as if he was absorbing every word, every nuance. His empathy was palpable, a balm to her conflicted soul, and she felt a connection forming between them, one that transcended the barriers of language and culture.

Eventually, the rain eased, and they stepped out of the gallery into the cool, damp night. The city was hushed, the streets glistening under the soft glow of streetlights, as if the rain had washed away the day's hustle and bustle, leaving behind a world that was calm and serene. Edward offered to walk her home, and she accepted, the two of them falling into an easy rhythm as they strolled through the quiet streets.

As they walked, Edward spoke of his philosophy on life that it was a journey, not a destination, and that the most important thing was to follow one's passions, regardless of what others might think. Li Wei listened, her heart heavy with the knowledge that she was at a crossroads. She had come to London to study, to broaden her horizons, but she had not anticipated the emotional journey she would embark upon. The city had awakened something in her a desire for independence, for self-discovery, and for the freedom to choose her own path.

When they finally reached her accommodation, they stood for a moment in the doorway, the night air crisp and cool around them. Edward smiled, his eyes warm and inviting, and Li Wei felt a flutter of something deep within her a mix of fear and excitement, of longing and uncertainty. She thanked him for the evening, and he nodded, his gaze lingering on her for a moment before he turned to leave.

As she watched him walk away, disappearing into the night, Li Wei felt a pang of loneliness, but also a sense of possibility. London was a city of infinite opportunities, a place where she could reinvent herself, explore new ideas, and perhaps, discover who she truly was. But it was also a city that would challenge her, force her to confront her deepest fears and desires, and ultimately, make her choose between the life she had always known and the life she had only just begun to imagine.

That night, as she lay in bed, listening to the soft patter of rain against the window, Li Wei's thoughts drifted between the past and the future, between the comfort of familiarity and the thrill of the unknown.

She knew that her journey was only beginning, and that the decisions she would make in the coming months would shape the rest of her life. But for now, she allowed herself to simply be in the moment, to savor the sweet taste of freedom and the tantalizing promise of what lay ahead.phony of voices that played a constant background melody. It was a stark reminder that she had indeed arrived in a different world. London this sprawling metropolis she had only known through books and movies was now her reality. The city represented more than just a place; it was a dream, a symbol of freedom, and the gateway to a life she had long envisioned. Here, in this foreign land, she could escape the confining expectations of her traditional upbringing in Guangzhou and embrace the endless possibilities of the West.

As she walked through the terminal, the clattering of trolleys and the rhythmic shuffle of footsteps created a kind of urban music. Li Wei moved like a thread through the fabric of the crowd, weaving her way through throngs of travelers, each with their own story, each a part of the intricate tapestry of the airport. She clutched the handle of her suitcase, her knuckles white against the cold metal, as if holding on to the last vestiges of the life she was leaving behind. Yet, even as she stepped forward, she couldn't shake the sensation that a part of her remained rooted in Guangzhou, tethered by invisible strings to the familiar and the known.

The cool, crisp air of London greeted her as she exited the terminal, a stark contrast to the humid warmth of her hometown. The city's atmosphere was different not just in temperature but in its very essence. The sky was a vast expanse of gray, clouds hanging low like a heavy quilt, as if threatening to engulf the city below. She inhaled deeply, the cold air filling her lungs with a sharpness that was both invigorating and unsettling. The air had a dampness to it, carrying with it the faint scent of rain-soaked earth and the distant aroma of brewing coffee from the airport cafés. She pulled her coat tighter around her slender frame, savoring the unfamiliar sensation of cold air nipping at her cheeks. It was as though the city was embracing her in its own cold, aloof way, and she welcomed the change, the sense of stepping into a new chapter of her life, even if it meant leaving behind everything she had known.

The taxi ride to her student accommodation was a blur of rain-slicked streets, red double-decker buses, and iconic black cabs. The windows were streaked with rain, the droplets chasing each other down the glass, blurring the outside world into a watercolor of gray and red. The buildings loomed over her, their old brick facades soaked in history, and she marveled at the seamless blend of the ancient and the modern. The taxi driver, a man with graying hair and a thick Cockney accent, made small talk as they drove through the city, but his words barely registered. Li Wei was too absorbed in the sights around her. The grandeur of London was overwhelming, the sheer scale of it all daunting. Yet, within the vastness, there was a sense of intimacy a feeling that each corner, each cobblestone, had a story to tell.

She caught glimpses of landmarks she had only seen in books or on the screen the Tower of London, its ancient stones whispering tales of the past; the Thames, winding its way through the city like a silver ribbon, its surface reflecting the brooding sky above; and the Houses of Parliament, with Big Ben standing tall, a sentinel watching over the capital. These were not just buildings or monuments; they were symbols of a history that stretched back centuries, a history that now, in some small way, she was becoming a part of.

Her accommodation was a modest room in a shared student house in Bloomsbury, not far from the British Museum. The house itself was old, its walls thick with stories of the students who had lived there before her. The bricks were weathered, the mortar between them cracked and uneven, as if time itself had pressed its weight upon the building. The wooden floors creaked underfoot as she made her way up the narrow staircase, the sound echoing through the otherwise silent house. The air was filled with the faint scent of musty books and damp wood, a smell that seemed to belong to another era. As she unpacked her suitcase, the weight of her journey began to settle on her shoulders. The photographs of her family, carefully placed on her desk, seemed to gaze back at her, their faces frozen in time, reminding her of the life she had temporarily left behind. Her mother had been tearful at the airport, clutching her hand and reminding her to eat well and study hard. Her father, though more composed, had a stern yet loving look in his eyes, as if to say, "Make us proud."

Her fiancé, Zhang Yufei, had been supportive of her decision to study abroad, yet his presence loomed large in her thoughts. Their families had arranged their engagement, a union meant to strengthen business ties between their fathers' companies. Yufei was kind, reliable, and everything her family desired for her. But was he what she wanted? Their last conversation before her departure had been a mixture of encouragement and underlying tension. Yufei had urged her to seize the opportunity, but she could see the flicker of uncertainty in his eyes, a shadow of doubt that mirrored her own. It was as though they both understood, without saying it, that this journey was not just about her education it was about discovering who she truly was, and perhaps, who she wanted to become.

As she settled into her new life at the University of London, Li Wei found solace in her studies. Her days were filled with lectures, library sessions, and the occasional sightseeing adventure with her new friends. The university's campus was a blend of historic buildings and modern facilities, a testament to its long-standing academic excellence. The grand old structures stood like sentinels of knowledge, their stone walls and ivy-covered facades exuding a sense of timelessness, while the newer buildings, with their sleek lines and modern architecture, represented the institution's forward-thinking spirit.

She marveled at the grandeur of the Senate House Library, its vast collection of books and manuscripts providing a treasure trove of knowledge. The library itself was a place of reverence, the silence within its walls almost tangible, broken only by the soft rustle of pages turning and the occasional cough. The high ceilings, adorned with intricate moldings, and the rows upon rows of bookshelves filled her with a sense of awe. Here, she could lose herself in the words of the greats, and perhaps, find a way to understand her own story. The scent of old paper and leather-bound volumes was intoxicating, a smell that carried the weight of history, of minds that had pondered the very questions she now grappled with.

Her fellow students were a diverse group, hailing from all corners of the globe. There was Amara from Nigeria, whose infectious laughter and boundless energy made her an instant friend. Amara was a whirlwind of enthusiasm, her presence a bright spot in the often gray London days. She had a way of making even the most mundane activities feel like an adventure, and her stories of life in Lagos were as vivid as the colorful prints she wore. Emily from Australia, with her easygoing demeanor and love for adventure, quickly became her travel buddy. Emily was a free spirit, her love for the outdoors and penchant for spontaneous road trips a stark contrast to Li Wei's more reserved nature. And then there was Rajesh from India, whose sharp intellect and thoughtful insights made him a valuable study partner. Rajesh was quiet, almost reserved, but when he spoke, his words carried weight. His knowledge of literature was vast, and their discussions often stretched late into the night, each pushing the other to think more deeply, more critically.

Despite the initial culture shock, Li Wei embraced the challenges of living in a foreign country. She learned to navigate the intricate web of the London Underground, its maze of tunnels and platforms a world unto itself. The rhythmic clatter of the trains, the rush of air as they approached, and the blur of faces passing by became familiar, comforting in their own way. She found her favorite local café, a small, tucked-away place where she could sip on a cup of Earl Grey while reading, the steam from the tea mingling with the aroma of freshly baked scones. The café became her sanctuary, a place where she could momentarily escape the pressures of her new life and lose herself in the words of Austen,

Brontë, and Woolf. The café's walls were lined with shelves of books, their spines worn and faded, each one a potential companion for her solitary afternoons.

She even began to appreciate the unpredictable weather, finding a strange comfort in the ever-present clouds and the way the rain seemed to cleanse the city, leaving the air fresh and cool. There was a rhythm to the weather, a kind of poetry in the way the rain would begin as a soft drizzle, almost imperceptible, before turning into a downpour that rattled against the windows. And then, just as suddenly, it would stop, leaving behind a world that glistened with the promise of renewal.

Her English improved rapidly, though she still found herself stumbling over idiomatic expressions and cultural references. It was in these moments, when she struggled to find the right words, that the distance between her old life and her new one seemed most pronounced. Yet, with each misstep, she grew more confident, her language skills a bridge between her past and her future. She became adept at reading between the lines, understanding the nuances of a language that was not her own, but was quickly becoming a part of her.

One evening, as she was returning from the library, her arms laden with books, she found herself caught in a sudden downpour. The rain was relentless, soaking through her clothes and plastering her hair to her head. She ducked into the nearest building for shelter, only to find herself in a small, dimly lit art gallery. The walls were adorned with paintings, their colors vibrant against the muted light. The air was thick with the scent of oil paint and varnish, a smell that reminded her of the art classes she had taken as a child. She wandered through the gallery, her wet shoes squeaking against the polished floor, the rain forgotten as she lost herself in the art around her.

It was here that she met Edward, a fellow student and art enthusiast. He was standing in front of a large canvas, his head tilted slightly as he studied the brushstrokes with a critical eye. Edward was tall, with unruly brown hair that fell into his eyes, and a demeanor that was both relaxed and intense. His clothes were rumpled, as if he had dressed in a hurry, and his fingers were stained with ink, a sign of his artistic pursuits. He turned to her as she approached, a smile playing on his lips as if he had been expecting her.

"You're soaked," he said with a chuckle, his accent a melodious mix of British and something else she couldn't quite place. There was warmth in his voice, a kind of easy charm that immediately put her at ease.

She smiled, brushing a strand of wet hair from her face. "It's London, I suppose," she replied, her own accent still carrying the soft lilt of Cantonese. There was something about him, a kind of magnetic pull that made her want to stay and talk, to learn more about this stranger who seemed so at ease in a world she was still navigating.

They struck up a conversation, initially about the art that surrounded them—the bold strokes of color, the subtle interplay of light and shadow, the way each piece seemed to tell its own story. Edward spoke passionately about his favorite artists, his words flowing like a river, full of energy and insight. He had a way of making the art come alive, of making her see it not just as images on a canvas, but as expressions of the soul. He was an artist himself, he explained, though he modestly downplayed his talents.

As the conversation deepened, they talked of more than just art. They spoke of life in London, of the challenges and joys of living in a city that was both welcoming and overwhelming. Edward had been born in England, but his mother was French, and he had spent much of his childhood moving between the two countries. His perspective on the world was shaped by this duality, by the blending of cultures that had become a part of who he was.

Li Wei found herself captivated by Edward's stories, by the way he spoke of the world with such passion and curiosity. He was unlike anyone she had ever met—free-spirited, creative, and unafraid to challenge the status quo. In him, she saw a reflection of the life she longed to lead, a life unbound by the expectations of others.

Yet, even as she felt herself drawn to Edward, a part of her held back, the weight of her engagement to Zhang Yufei pressing down on her like a heavy cloak. The memory of their last conversation lingered in her mind, a reminder of the life she had left behind in Guangzhou. Yufei was everything her family wanted for her—stable, reliable, and deeply rooted in their shared culture. But in the presence of Edward, she couldn't help but question whether stability and reliability were enough.

As they stood in the gallery, the rain still pounding against the windows, Li Wei felt a strange sense of contentment. She was in a foreign city, far from home, surrounded by strangers and uncertainties, and yet, for the first time in a long while, she felt a spark of something new—something that had been missing in her life. Was it the thrill of the unknown? The allure of possibility? Or was it simply the joy of being herself, free from the expectations that had always defined her?

As the evening wore on, the conversation between Li Wei and Edward meandered through various topics, each one revealing more about their personalities and the lives they had led up to this point. Edward spoke of his travels through Europe, his love for the art of the Renaissance, and his belief that life was meant to be lived passionately and fully. He was studying fine arts at the university, but his true love was painting—an expression of his innermost thoughts and emotions. He showed her a sketchbook he carried with him, its pages filled with quick, expressive drawings that captured moments of beauty and emotion in a way words could not.

Li Wei found herself sharing more than she had intended—about her life in Guangzhou, her family's expectations, and the burden of an engagement she hadn't truly chosen. Edward listened with a quiet intensity, his gaze never leaving her face as she spoke, as if he was absorbing every word, every nuance. His empathy was palpable, a balm to her conflicted soul, and she felt a connection forming between them, one that transcended the barriers of language and culture.

Eventually, the rain eased, and they stepped out of the gallery into the cool, damp night. The city was hushed, the streets glistening under the soft glow of streetlights, as if the rain had washed away the day's hustle and bustle, leaving behind a world that was calm and serene. Edward offered to walk her home, and she accepted, the two of them falling into an easy rhythm as they strolled through the quiet streets.

As they walked, Edward spoke of his philosophy on life that it was a journey, not a destination, and that the most important thing was to follow one's passions, regardless of what others might think. Li Wei listened, her heart heavy with the knowledge that she was at a crossroads. She had come to London to study, to broaden her horizons, but she had not anticipated the emotional journey she would embark upon. The city had awakened something in her a desire for independence, for self-discovery, and for the freedom to choose her own path.

When they finally reached her accommodation, they stood for a moment in the doorway, the night air crisp and cool around them. Edward smiled, his eyes warm and inviting, and Li Wei felt a flutter of something deep within her a mix of fear and excitement, of longing and uncertainty. She thanked him for the evening, and he nodded, his gaze lingering on her for a moment before he turned to leave.

As she watched him walk away, disappearing into the night, Li Wei felt a pang of loneliness, but also a sense of possibility. London was a city of infinite opportunities, a place where she could reinvent herself, explore new ideas, and perhaps, discover who she truly was. But it was also a city that would challenge her, force her to confront her deepest fears and desires, and ultimately, make her choose between the life she had always known and the life she had only just begun to imagine.

That night, as she lay in bed, listening to the soft patter of rain against the window, Li Wei's thoughts drifted between the past and the future, between the comfort of familiarity and the thrill of the unknown. She knew that her journey was only beginning, and that the decisions she would make in the coming months would shape the rest of her life. But for now, she allowed herself to simply be in the moment, to savor the sweet taste of freedom and the tantalizing promise of what lay ahead.

Chapter 2: The Encounter

Settling into her new life at the University of London, Li Wei found solace in her studies, yet the vastness of the city and the whirlwind of new experiences often left her feeling like a small, solitary figure in a grand painting. The campus itself, a harmonious blend of historic stonework and modern glass facades, stood as a symbol of the university's long-standing academic excellence. Each building seemed to tell a story, its walls whispering the tales of scholars and intellectuals who had walked the same paths long before her. The cobblestone streets, shaded by ancient oaks, were alive with the footsteps of students hurrying to lectures or pausing to chat beneath the golden foliage of a London autumn.

Li Wei quickly found her rhythm in this new world, her days meticulously structured around lectures, endless hours in the library, and the occasional sightseeing adventure with her new friends. The Senate House Library became her sanctuary, its towering shelves crammed with books from every conceivable field of study. She often lost herself in the labyrinth of knowledge, running her fingers along the spines of well-worn volumes, each promising a new journey into the past.

Her fellow students were a kaleidoscope of cultures and backgrounds, each bringing a unique perspective to their shared academic endeavors. There was Amara from Nigeria, whose infectious laughter echoed through the halls and whose boundless energy seemed to light up even the gloomiest London day. Amara's vibrant storytelling about her homeland, with its lush landscapes and rich traditions, often captivated Li Wei, transporting her to a world so different from her own.

Emily from Australia was another fast friend. With her sun-kissed skin and easygoing demeanor, she brought a breath of the Outback into the urban sprawl of London. Emily's love for adventure was infectious, and it wasn't long before the two of them were planning weekend escapades to explore the city's hidden gems from the bustling markets of Camden to the quiet serenity of Hampstead Heath.

Rajesh, a thoughtful and introspective student from India, often joined their group, his sharp intellect and deep insights making him a valuable study partner. Rajesh had a way of seeing the world that was both poetic and pragmatic, often quoting from ancient Indian texts to explain modern dilemmas. His presence was calming, a counterbalance to the often chaotic energy of university life.

One crisp autumn evening, as the wind carried with it the first hint of winter's chill, Li Wei decided to attend a meeting of the university's literary society. It was held in a cozy, dimly lit room in one of the older, more secluded buildings on campus. The heavy oak doors creaked as she pushed them open, and she was greeted by the comforting scent of old books and the low murmur of voices engaged in animated discussion. The room was warm, almost too warm, a sharp contrast to the biting cold outside, and Li Wei immediately felt the tension in her shoulders ease.

The society had a reputation for being a haven for passionate readers and writers, a place where ideas were exchanged freely, and Li Wei hoped to find kindred spirits among its members. The room was filled with students, their faces illuminated by the warm glow of table lamps that cast long shadows across the walls lined with bookshelves. The flickering light gave the room an almost ethereal quality, as though it existed outside the constraints of time.

The society's president, Professor Harrison, was an imposing figure, his tall frame draped in a tweed jacket that had clearly seen many winters. His deep, resonant voice commanded attention, yet his eyes, bright with curiosity, softened his otherwise stern appearance. As he welcomed Li Wei, he inquired about her background and interests with genuine interest, his voice carrying the authority of someone who had dedicated his life to literature.

"Welcome, Li Wei. It's always a pleasure to have new members join us," he said, extending his hand with a firm but warm grip. His gaze was steady, as though he could see right through to her soul. "Tell us, what brings you to our literary haven?"

Li Wei smiled shyly, feeling the weight of the room's attention on her. "I'm here to pursue a Master's degree in English Literature. I've always loved reading and writing, and I thought this society would be the perfect place to connect with others who share my passion."

Professor Harrison's smile widened, revealing a hint of satisfaction. "You're in the right place," he replied, his voice a rich baritone that seemed to resonate with the very walls of the room. "Please, make yourself at home. We're just about to start our discussion on the works of Charles Dickens."

Li Wei found a seat near the back, her excitement growing as she listened to the spirited debate unfolding around her. The members dissected Dickens' novels with a fervor that bordered on reverence, discussing his portrayal of social class, the plight of the poor, and the complexities of his characters. As she absorbed their words, Li Wei felt a familiar warmth spreading through her chest a recognition of the power of literature to connect minds and bridge the vast distances between cultures.

During a break in the discussion, Li Wei noticed a young man seated across from her. His disarming smile seemed to reach his eyes, which crinkled slightly at the corners in a way that made him look both kind and approachable. There was something about him that put her at ease, a quiet confidence that made her feel comfortable in his presence. He introduced himself as Edward, an English major working on his thesis about the influence of Victorian literature on modern storytelling.

"Hello, Li Wei," he said, his voice warm and inviting, like the first sip of a well-brewed cup of tea on a cold day. "I couldn't help but notice how engaged you were during the discussion. What do you think of Dickens' portrayal of social class?"

Li Wei hesitated for a moment, her mind racing to organize her thoughts. She had always been more comfortable expressing herself through writing than speaking, but there was something about Edward's genuine curiosity that made her feel safe. "I think Dickens does an incredible job of highlighting the struggles of the lower class while also exposing the hypocrisies of the upper class. His characters are so vivid and complex, and I believe his work is still relevant today, especially when we look at the ongoing issues of inequality in our world."

Edward's eyes lit up with interest, the light from the nearby lamp reflecting off his glasses. "I couldn't agree more. It's fascinating how his themes resonate with modern audiences. Have you read 'Great Expectations'?"

"Yes, it's one of my favorites," Li Wei answered, her voice gaining confidence as she spoke about something she loved. "I love the way he explores Pip's journey and the moral dilemmas he faces. There's something so human about his struggle to reconcile his desires with his sense of right and wrong."

Their conversation flowed effortlessly, like a stream winding its way through a forest, covering a range of topics from literature to cultural differences and personal experiences. Edward was genuinely interested in learning about Li Wei's background and her life in China. He listened attentively as she shared stories of her childhood in Guangzhou, her family's traditions, and the journey that had brought her to London.

As the evening wore on, the room began to empty, but Li Wei and Edward continued to talk, their voices growing softer as the night deepened. Li Wei found herself drawn to Edward's easygoing nature and genuine interest in her culture. He was unlike anyone she had met before—his curiosity was free of the exoticism she had often encountered when people asked about her background. Instead, he seemed to want to understand her on a deeper level, as a person rather than a symbol of another culture.

Despite the growing attraction, a nagging guilt tugged at her every time she thought of Yufei back in China. She had promised herself that she would honor the engagement, that she would return to him when her studies were complete. But the connection she felt with Edward was undeniable, and she was torn between duty and desire, tradition and the pull of her own heart.

After the meeting, Edward offered to walk Li Wei back to her accommodation. The crisp night air was invigorating, and the sky was clear, the stars twinkling like diamonds against the velvet blackness. As they strolled through the quiet streets of Bloomsbury, their footsteps echoing in the stillness, their conversation continued uninterrupted.

"Thank you for tonight, Edward. I had a wonderful time," Li Wei said as they reached her doorstep, her voice soft with the weight of the evening's revelations.

"The pleasure was mine," Edward replied, his smile warm and genuine. "I'm glad we met, Li Wei. I hope we can do this again sometime."

Li Wei nodded, her heart fluttering with a mixture of excitement and trepidation. "I'd like that."

In the days that followed, Li Wei and Edward's paths seemed to cross with increasing frequency, as though fate had decided to weave their lives together. They attended more literary society meetings, their debates growing more animated as they challenged each other's views, yet always with a respect that deepened their bond. Outside of the society, they began to explore the city together, discovering new places and creating memories that Li Wei knew she would carry with her forever.

One Saturday afternoon, Edward invited Li Wei to visit the British Library. The imposing building, with its modernist architecture, housed one of the largest collections of books and manuscripts in the world. For Li Wei, it was a dream come true a place where she could lose herself in the pages of history and literature.

As they wandered through the library's vast halls, Edward pointed out some of the rare and valuable items on display, including the Magna Carta, with its faded ink and fragile parchment, and original manuscripts by famous authors, their handwriting a window into the minds that had shaped literature. Li Wei was particularly captivated by the handwritten notes of Virginia Woolf, the loops and curves of her pen strokes giving life to the thoughts of one of her literary idols.

In one of the quieter reading rooms, surrounded by the soft rustle of turning pages and the gentle hum of the library's air conditioning, Edward handed Li Wei a book he had picked out for her. It was an old, leather-bound copy of 'Jane Eyre' by Charlotte Brontë, its pages yellowed with age, the edges worn soft from countless readings.

"I thought you might like this," Edward said, his voice hushed in the reverent silence of the library.

Li Wei took the book from him, her fingers tracing the intricate design on the cover. "Thank you, Edward. This means a lot to me."

As she opened the book and began to read, Edward watched her, a soft smile playing on his lips. In that moment, surrounded by the timeless wisdom of the library, Li Wei felt a sense of contentment she hadn't experienced in a long time. The world outside might be vast and overwhelming, but here, in this sanctuary of knowledge, she had found a connection that transcended the boundaries of culture and geography.

But even as she reveled in the joy of this new friendship, Li Wei could not shake the thought of Yufei. The memory of his face, his voice, the promises they had made to each other, lingered in the back of her mind like a shadow, reminding her of the life she had left behind.

That night, as she lay in bed, staring at the ceiling, Li Wei found herself at a crossroads. Her heart was pulling her in two directions toward the familiar comfort of the past and the exciting, uncertain possibilities of the future. She knew she had to make a choice, but the weight of that decision pressed down on her, leaving her feeling trapped between two worlds.

The city outside her window was alive with the sounds of a Saturday night—cars honking, people laughing, the distant thrum of music from a nearby club. But inside her small room, all was silent, save for the rapid beating of her heart. Li Wei closed her eyes, willing herself to sleep, but the question of what to do next loomed large in her mind, refusing to be silenced.

Settling into her new life at the University of London, Li Wei quickly found solace in her studies. Her days were filled with lectures, library sessions, and the occasional sightseeing adventure with her new friends. The campus, a blend of historic buildings and modern facilities, was a testament to the university's long-standing academic excellence. Li Wei marveled at the grandeur of the Senate House Library, its vast collection of books and manuscripts providing a treasure trove of knowledge.

Her fellow students were a diverse group, hailing from all corners of the globe. There was Amara from Nigeria, whose infectious laughter and boundless energy made her an instant friend. Emily from Australia, with her easygoing demeanor and love for adventure, quickly became her travel buddy. And then there was Rajesh from India, whose sharp intellect and thoughtful insights made him a valuable study partner.

One crisp autumn evening, Li Wei decided to attend a meeting of the university's literary society. It was held in a cozy, dimly lit room in one of the older buildings on campus. The society had a reputation for being a gathering place for passionate readers and writers, and Li Wei hoped to find kindred spirits among its members.

As she entered the room, she was greeted by the sight of students engaged in animated discussions, their faces illuminated by the warm glow of table lamps. The society's president, Professor Harrison, was an imposing figure with a deep, resonant voice that commanded attention. He welcomed Li Wei warmly, his eyes twinkling with curiosity as he asked about her background and interests.

"Welcome, Li Wei. It's always a pleasure to have new members join us," he said, extending his hand. "Tell us, what brings you to our literary haven?"

Li Wei smiled shyly, shaking his hand. "I'm here to pursue a Master's degree in English Literature. I've always loved reading and writing, and I thought this society would be the perfect place to connect with others who share my passion."

"You're in the right place," Professor Harrison replied, his smile widening. "Please, make yourself at home. We're just about to start our discussion on the works of Charles Dickens."

Li Wei found a seat and settled in, her excitement growing as she listened to the spirited debate unfolding around her. The members discussed the social and political themes in Dickens' novels, dissecting his characters and exploring the intricacies of his storytelling. Li Wei found herself drawn into the conversation, her own thoughts and opinions bubbling to the surface.

During a break in the discussion, a young man seated across from her caught her eye. He had a disarming smile and a way of making everyone around him feel at ease. He introduced himself as Edward, an English major working on his thesis about the influence of Victorian literature on modern storytelling.

"Hello, Li Wei," he said, his voice warm and inviting. "I couldn't help but notice how engaged you were during the discussion. What do you think of Dickens' portrayal of social class?"

Li Wei hesitated for a moment, then replied, "I think Dickens does an incredible job of highlighting the struggles of the lower class while also exposing the hypocrisies of the upper class. His characters are so vivid and complex, and I believe his work is still relevant today."

Edward's eyes lit up with interest. "I couldn't agree more. It's fascinating how his themes resonate with modern audiences. Have you read 'Great Expectations'?"

"Yes, it's one of my favorites," Li Wei answered, her excitement growing. "I love the way he explores Pip's journey and the moral dilemmas he faces."

Their conversation flowed effortlessly, covering a range of topics from literature to cultural differences and personal experiences. Edward was genuinely interested in learning about Li Wei's background and her life in China. He listened attentively as she shared stories of her childhood in Guangzhou, her family's traditions, and her journey to London.

As the evening progressed, Li Wei found herself drawn to Edward's easygoing nature and genuine interest in her culture. He was unlike anyone she had met before, and she felt a connection with him that she couldn't quite explain. Despite the growing attraction, a nagging guilt tugged at her every time she thought of Yufei back in China.

After the meeting, Edward offered to walk Li Wei back to her accommodation. The crisp night air was invigorating, and they strolled through the quiet streets of Bloomsbury, their conversation continuing uninterrupted.

"Thank you for tonight, Edward. I had a wonderful time," Li Wei said as they reached her doorstep.

"The pleasure was mine," Edward replied with a smile. "I'm glad we met, Li Wei. I hope we can do this again sometime."

Li Wei nodded, her heart fluttering with anticipation. "I'd like that."

In the days that followed, Li Wei and Edward's paths continued to cross. They attended more literary society meetings together, sharing their thoughts and opinions on various works of literature. They began to spend more time outside of the society as well, exploring the city together and discovering new places.

One Saturday afternoon, Edward invited Li Wei to visit the British Library. The imposing building housed one of the largest collections of books and manuscripts in the world, and Li Wei was eager to see it.

As they wandered through the library's vast halls, Edward pointed out some of the rare and valuable items on display, including the Magna Carta and original manuscripts by famous authors.

"This place is incredible," Li Wei said, her eyes wide with wonder. "I could spend days here and still not see everything."

"I know the feeling," Edward replied with a chuckle. "It's one of my favorite places in the city. There's something magical about being surrounded by so much history and knowledge."

They found a quiet corner in the library and settled down with a stack of books. Li Wei lost herself in the pages of a rare edition of Jane Austen's "Pride and Prejudice," while Edward immersed himself in a collection of Victorian poetry.

As they read, Li Wei felt a sense of contentment wash over her. She was beginning to find her place in this new world, and Edward's presence made the transition easier. She enjoyed his company and the way he made her feel valued, understood, and appreciated.

One evening, after a particularly engaging literary society meeting, Edward invited Li Wei to a small café near campus. The café was cozy and intimate, with soft lighting and a warm atmosphere. They found a table by the window and ordered cups of hot chocolate.

As they sipped their drinks, Edward leaned forward, his expression serious yet tender.

"Li Wei, there's something I need to tell you," he began, his voice earnest. "I've come to care for you deeply. You're an amazing person, and I feel a connection with you that I've never felt with anyone else."

Li Wei's heart skipped a beat, her mind racing. She had been trying to deny her feelings for Edward, but hearing him voice his emotions made it impossible to ignore the truth.

"I care for you too, Edward," she whispered, her voice trembling. "But I'm engaged. My family has arranged a marriage for me with a man back in China."

Edward's eyes filled with a mixture of sadness and determination. "I understand your situation, and I don't want to pressure you. But I believe we have something special. You deserve to follow your heart and be happy."

Tears welled up in Li Wei's eyes as she grappled with her conflicting emotions. She wanted to be with Edward, to embrace this new love, but her sense of duty and loyalty to Yufei held her back.

"I don't know what to do," she admitted, her voice barely above a whisper.

Edward reached across the table and took her hand, his touch warm and reassuring. "Whatever you decide, I'll support you. But know that you have a choice, Li Wei. You deserve to be happy."

As they left the café and walked back to her accommodation, Li Wei's mind was a whirlwind of thoughts and emotions. She knew she had difficult decisions to make, but she also felt a glimmer of hope.

Chapter 3: The Cultural Divide

The early days of autumn in London brought with them a crispness in the air, a subtle reminder that the warm, golden days of summer were now in the past. The leaves on the trees in the park near Edward and Li Wei's flat had begun to turn shades of amber and crimson, creating a picturesque scene that seemed to glow under the soft afternoon sunlight.

Despite the beauty around them, Li Wei couldn't shake the feeling of unease that had settled in her chest. She sat on a bench in the park, watching as a group of children played nearby, their laughter echoing through the cool air. Edward was beside her, his hand resting gently on hers, but even his reassuring presence couldn't completely dispel the sense of isolation she felt.

"Is something bothering you?" Edward's voice broke the silence, his tone gentle and concerned. He had noticed the change in her demeanor over the past few days, and it worried him.

Li Wei hesitated for a moment, unsure of how to express the complex emotions swirling within her. She had always prided herself on her independence and strength, but being in a foreign country, so far from everything familiar, was beginning to take its toll.

"It's just... I don't know," she finally said, her voice soft and uncertain. "Sometimes I feel like I don't belong here, like there's this... divide between me and everything around me."

Edward frowned slightly, his brow furrowing in thought. "What do you mean?"

Li Wei took a deep breath, trying to find the right words. "It's hard to explain. It's like... there are so many little things, things that people here take for granted, that are so different from what I'm used to. And it's not just the big things, like the language or the customs. It's the small things, too. Like the way people greet each other, or the way they eat, or even how they think about time. It's all so different."

Edward nodded, his expression thoughtful. "I can see how that would be difficult. But isn't that part of the experience? Part of what makes living abroad so interesting?"

Li Wei looked down at their intertwined hands, her heart heavy. "I thought so too. But now... I'm not so sure. Sometimes it feels like I'm losing a part of myself, like I'm being stretched in so many directions that I don't know who I am anymore."

Edward was silent for a moment, his gaze fixed on her face as he considered her words. He had always admired Li Wei's strength and resilience, but he had also seen the quiet vulnerability beneath her calm exterior. He knew that moving to London had been a huge step for her, and he didn't want her to feel like she had to face these challenges alone.

"Li Wei," he said softly, his voice full of warmth and understanding. "You don't have to go through this on your own. I'm here with you, and I want to help you in any way I can. We're in this together, remember?"

Li Wei smiled weakly, grateful for his support but still feeling the weight of her own insecurities. "I know, Edward. And I'm so lucky to have you. But sometimes I wonder if... if maybe I'm not strong enough to handle all of this."

Edward shook his head firmly, his expression resolute. "Don't ever think that. You are one of the strongest people I know. You've already come so far, and you've faced so many challenges. This is just another one, and I know you can overcome it."

Li Wei nodded, though her heart still felt heavy. She wanted to believe him, but the doubts continued to gnaw at her. The cultural differences between her and the world around her felt like an invisible barrier, one that she wasn't sure she could ever fully break through.

Over the next few days, the sense of alienation only grew. At the university, Li Wei found herself struggling to keep up with the rapid pace of her classes, where the teaching style was so different from what she had been used to in China. The professors expected a level of independence and critical thinking that felt overwhelming, and she often found herself second-guessing her abilities.

Even simple interactions with her classmates left her feeling out of place. During lunch breaks, she would often find herself sitting quietly on the edges of conversations, unable to fully engage with the others. They would talk about things that she had little experience with—Western pop culture references, childhood memories that she couldn't relate to, or social norms that were unfamiliar to her.

One day, as she sat in the university cafeteria, picking at her lunch, a group of her classmates approached her table. They were friendly and welcoming, their smiles warm and genuine, but Li Wei couldn't shake the feeling of being an outsider.

"Hey, Li Wei!" one of them, a girl named Emma, said brightly. "We're going to a pub tonight after class. You should come with us!"

Li Wei hesitated, her mind racing. She had never been to a pub before, and the idea of spending the evening in a noisy, crowded place filled her with anxiety. But she didn't want to seem unfriendly or uninterested.

"I... I'm not sure," she stammered, feeling the pressure of their expectant gazes. "I've got a lot of studying to do..."

"Oh, come on!" another classmate, Tom, chimed in. "You've got to take a break some time! It'll be fun, I promise."

Li Wei forced a smile, but inside, she felt a pang of dread. The thought of trying to fit in, of trying to navigate the unfamiliar social dynamics of a pub, was daunting. She could already imagine the awkwardness, the feeling of not knowing what to say or how to act.

But before she could decline, Edward's words from the park echoed in her mind: "You are one of the strongest people I know." She took a deep breath, summoning her courage.

"Okay," she said finally, her voice steady. "I'll come."

That evening, as they walked to the pub, Li Wei tried to push her fears aside. The cool night air was refreshing, and the streets were bustling with activity. Edward had been supportive when she told him about the outing, encouraging her to step out of her comfort zone and assuring her that she would do just fine.

But when they arrived at the pub, Li Wei felt her heart sink. The place was crowded and noisy, filled with the sound of laughter, clinking glasses, and lively conversation. The air was thick with the scent of beer and food, and the dim lighting made it difficult to see clearly.

As they found a table and sat down, Li Wei felt a wave of discomfort wash over her. The noise, the unfamiliar smells, the chaotic energy of the place it was all overwhelming. Her classmates seemed at ease, chatting and laughing as they ordered drinks, but Li Wei felt out of place, as if she were an observer rather than a participant.

When it came time to order, she was unsure of what to choose. The drink menu was filled with unfamiliar names, and she didn't know what any of them tasted like. She hesitated, her eyes scanning the list, but nothing seemed to make sense.

"What are you going to have, Li Wei?" Emma asked, smiling encouragingly.

Li Wei glanced at the menu again, feeling a flush of embarrassment. "I'm not sure... I've never had any of these before."

Tom chuckled good-naturedly. "Don't worry, we'll help you out. How about trying a cider? It's sweet and not too strong."

Li Wei nodded, grateful for the suggestion. "Okay, that sounds good."

When her drink arrived, she took a tentative sip. The taste was unfamiliar, but not unpleasant. She forced herself to smile, hoping to mask her discomfort.

As the evening wore on, Li Wei tried to engage in the conversation, but it was difficult. Her classmates talked about topics that were foreign to her, and she found it hard to follow along. She felt like an outsider, struggling to keep up with the flow of the conversation.

At one point, Tom made a joke that sent the table into fits of laughter. Li Wei smiled politely, but the joke had gone over her head. She felt a pang of isolation, a reminder of the cultural divide that separated her from the others.

When the evening finally came to an end, Li Wei felt a mixture of relief and disappointment. She had made an effort to fit in, but it had been exhausting, and she couldn't shake the feeling that she didn't belong.

As she walked home, the streets quiet and empty, she replayed the evening in her mind. The experience had been challenging, but she had pushed through it, and for that, she was proud of herself. But the sense of alienation still lingered, a reminder that she was living in a world that was different from her own.

When she finally arrived at the flat, Edward was waiting for her, his expression filled with concern.

"How was it?" he asked, his voice gentle.

Li Wei sighed, sinking onto the couch. "It was... okay. I tried my best, but it was hard. I just feel so out of place sometimes."

Edward sat down beside her, wrapping his arm around her shoulders. "I know it's not easy, Li Wei. But you're doing great. You're trying, and that's what matters."

Li Wei leaned into him, grateful for his support. "I just wish it wasn't so hard. I feel like I'm always on the outside, looking in."

Edward kissed her forehead, his touch warm and comforting. "You're not alone in this.

Chapter 4: Unspoken Tensions

The following weeks passed in a blur for Li Wei. The initial excitement of her new life in London had given way to a routine that was both comforting and, at times, suffocating. She continued to attend her classes, study diligently, and occasionally join her classmates for social outings, but the sense of unease that had begun to creep into her life showed no signs of abating.

Edward, ever the supportive partner, noticed the changes in her but struggled to find a way to help. He knew that Li Wei was grappling with more than just the usual challenges of adapting to a new environment. There was something deeper, something that neither of them could quite articulate.

One chilly afternoon, as they walked through the streets of London, the unspoken tensions between them finally began to surface.

"Do you ever miss home?" Li Wei asked, her voice quiet and tentative. The question had been on her mind for days, but she had been hesitant to voice it. She wasn't sure if she was seeking reassurance or simply trying to understand her own emotions.

Edward glanced at her, his brow furrowing slightly. "Of course I do," he replied, his tone thoughtful. "But I've been here for so long now that this feels like home too. Why do you ask?"

Li Wei shrugged, her gaze fixed on the pavement as they walked. "I don't know. I guess... I've been thinking a lot about it lately. About what it means to call a place home."

Edward slowed his pace, sensing that there was more to her words than she was letting on. "Do you miss China?" he asked gently.

Li Wei nodded, a lump forming in her throat. "Yes, I do. I miss my family, my friends, the food, the language... everything. It's hard sometimes, being so far away from all of that."

Edward stopped walking, turning to face her. His expression was full of concern and love, but also a hint of something else something that Li

Wei couldn't quite place. "I understand," he said softly. "But you know you can talk to me about anything, right? I'm here for you."

Li Wei smiled weakly, appreciating his words but still feeling the weight of her own unspoken fears. "I know, Edward. And I'm so grateful for that. But... sometimes I feel like there's this huge gap between us. Like we're living in two different worlds."

Edward's expression darkened slightly, a flicker of frustration crossing his face. "What do you mean by that?"

Li Wei hesitated, unsure of how to explain the complicated emotions swirling within her. "It's just... there are so many things that are different between us. Our cultures, our backgrounds, the way we see the world... Sometimes it feels like we're speaking two different languages, even when we're not."

Edward frowned, his tone growing more serious. "But we've always known that, haven't we? We knew from the beginning that our relationship would have challenges because of our different backgrounds. But I thought we were strong enough to overcome them."

Li Wei nodded, her heart heavy with conflicting emotions. "I thought so too. But lately... I don't know. I feel like I'm losing a part of myself, and I don't know how to hold on to it."

Edward's frustration deepened, though he tried to keep his voice calm. "Are you saying that being with me is causing you to lose yourself?"

Li Wei's eyes widened in alarm, realizing how her words might have sounded. "No, Edward, that's not what I mean. I love you, and I wouldn't change anything about our relationship. It's just... it's hard to find a balance between who I was and who I'm becoming."

Edward sighed, running a hand through his hair. He had always known that their relationship would face obstacles, but hearing Li Wei voice her doubts brought a new level of anxiety that he hadn't anticipated. "I don't want you to feel like you're losing yourself, Li Wei. But I also don't know how to help you if you don't tell me what's really going on."

Li Wei looked away, her eyes stinging with unshed tears. She had never wanted to burden Edward with her struggles, but now she wondered if keeping them to herself had only made things worse.

"It's not your fault," she said softly, her voice barely above a whisper. "It's just... everything feels so overwhelming sometimes. The cultural differences, the pressure to succeed, the loneliness... I'm trying to figure it all out, but it's hard."

Edward reached out, gently cupping her face in his hands. "You don't have to figure it out alone, Li Wei. We're a team, remember? We can work through this together."

Li Wei leaned into his touch, drawing comfort from his warmth, but the doubts lingered in the back of her mind. Could they really overcome the challenges that seemed to be pulling them apart? Or were the differences between them too great to bridge?

That evening, as they sat in their small flat, the tension between them hung heavy in the air. They tried to distract themselves with dinner and a movie, but the unresolved conversation from earlier continued to gnaw at both of them.

As the movie played on the screen, Edward's thoughts drifted back to their earlier conversation. He had always prided himself on being open-minded and understanding, but now he couldn't help but feel a pang of insecurity. Was he enough for Li Wei? Was their love strong enough to withstand the cultural divide that seemed to be growing between them?

Li Wei, too, was lost in her thoughts. She couldn't shake the feeling that she was failing—failing to adapt, failing to communicate, failing to find her place in this new world. She loved Edward deeply, but the fear that their differences might eventually tear them apart was becoming harder to ignore.

As the credits rolled and the movie came to an end, Edward turned to Li Wei, his expression serious. "We need to talk," he said, his voice firm but gentle.

Li Wei nodded, bracing herself for what was to come. She knew that they couldn't continue to ignore the issues that were brewing between them, but the thought of confronting them head-on filled her with dread.

Edward took a deep breath, searching for the right words. "Li Wei, I love you more than anything, and I want us to be happy together. But I can't help but feel like there's something you're not telling me. If we're going to make this work, we need to be honest with each other."

Li Wei looked into his eyes, seeing the love and concern reflected there. She knew that he was right, that they needed to be open and honest if they were going to navigate the challenges ahead. But the fear of losing him, of pushing him away with her doubts and insecurities, made her hesitate.

"I'm scared," she admitted finally, her voice trembling. "I'm scared that I'm not strong enough to handle all of this. That I'm going to lose myself, or worse, that I'm going to lose you."

Edward's heart ached at her words, and he pulled her into a tight embrace. "You're not going to lose me, Li Wei. I'm here, and I'm not going anywhere. We'll figure this out together, one step at a time."

Li Wei clung to him, her tears finally spilling over. She wanted to believe him, to trust that their love would be enough to overcome the obstacles in their path. But the fear of the unknown, of the challenges that still lay ahead, was a heavy burden to bear.

As they held each other in the quiet of their flat, the unspoken tensions between them remained. The road ahead was uncertain, and the cultural divide between them was real. But for now, they had each other, and that was a start.

Chapter 5: The Dilemma

Li Wei's days in London gradually fell into a rhythm, an intricate dance between the demands of academia and the blossoming connection she shared with Edward. Mornings were consumed by lectures and discussions in the historic lecture halls of her university, where the air buzzed with intellectual fervor. Afternoons were often spent in the vast, hushed expanse of the library, surrounded by the comforting scent of aged paper and the silent companionship of fellow students. But it was the evenings, those precious hours with Edward, that she cherished most. Each day, their bond deepened, weaving together threads of intellectual curiosity, mutual respect, and an affection that felt both exhilarating and terrifying.

Yet, beneath the surface of this burgeoning happiness, a storm brewed in Li Wei's heart. Her engagement to Yufei, a promise made to honor her family's wishes, hung over her like a shadow. The weight of her family's expectations pressed heavily upon her, a constant reminder of the life she was meant to lead, a life that seemed increasingly at odds with the one she was living in London.

London, with its eclectic blend of tradition and modernity, had become a playground for Li Wei and Edward's explorations. One evening, they found themselves wandering through the vibrant streets of Covent Garden. The cobblestone pathways echoed with the lively melodies of street performers, their music mingling with the laughter of tourists and locals alike. The air was thick with the scent of street food, a tantalizing mix of spices and fried delights that created a sensory tapestry of the city's bustling life.

As they wandered past the performers jugglers, violinists, and magicians who seemed to capture the very essence of London's spirit Edward turned to Li Wei, his eyes sparkling with a mischievous glint. "Have you ever tried fish and chips?" he asked, a playful smile tugging at the corners of his mouth.

Li Wei shook her head, her lips curving into a smile that mirrored his. "No, but I've heard it's a quintessential British experience."

Edward's grin widened. "Well, that simply won't do. Come on, let's remedy that right now."

They made their way to a nearby vendor, where the aroma of frying fish wafted through the air, mingling with the salty tang of the Thames in the distance. The vendor handed them a parcel wrapped in newspaper, the paper quickly growing translucent from the oil of the freshly fried meal. They found a bench near the piazza, where they could watch the performers while they ate.

Li Wei took her first bite, savoring the crunch of the batter and the tender flakiness of the fish beneath. "This is really good," she murmured, her eyes widening in surprise and delight.

Edward chuckled, pleased by her reaction. "I'm glad you like it. It's one of those simple pleasures that you can't miss while you're here."

As they shared the meal, their conversation flowed easily, as it always did. They spoke of literature, delving into the works of Shakespeare and Austen, and debated the merits of British versus Chinese poetry. Their discussions were often peppered with laughter, moments of understanding that required no words, and the occasional, thoughtful silence that spoke of a deepening connection.

Edward shared stories from his childhood, painting a vivid picture of life in a small village nestled in the English countryside. He spoke of the rolling hills and the ancient stone cottages, the sound of church bells on a Sunday morning, and the way the mist clung to the fields at dawn. Li Wei, in turn, told him about her life in Guangzhou the vibrant markets, the towering skyscrapers, and the deep-rooted traditions that shaped her family's daily life. She spoke of the festivals, where the streets would be awash in color and music, and of her grandmother's wisdom, passed down through stories told in the flickering candlelight.

One evening, as they strolled along the embankment of the Thames, the river glistening under the moonlight, Edward paused. He turned to

Li Wei, his expression earnest and his voice gentle. "Li Wei, I know this is difficult for you. But I want you to know that whatever happens, I'm here for you. You don't have to go through this alone."

His words, spoken with such sincerity, touched something deep within Li Wei. She looked into his eyes, searching for the truth she already knew was there, and found it. The storm in her heart raged on, but in Edward's gaze, she found a shelter, a place of calm amidst the chaos.

"Thank you, Edward," she whispered, her voice trembling with the weight of her emotions. "I appreciate it more than you know."

In the following weeks, Li Wei threw herself into her studies with renewed vigor. She sought solace in the structured predictability of her academic routine, hoping it would quiet the storm within her. The days became a blur of lectures, essays, and endless readings, but no matter how busy she kept herself, thoughts of Yufei and her family's expectations lingered at the edges of her mind, refusing to be ignored.

Yet, as much as she tried to focus on her studies, it was her evenings with Edward that became her true refuge. Together, they explored every corner of the city. They wandered through the echoing halls of the British Museum, marveled at the masterpieces in the National Gallery, and stood in awe before the grandeur of St. Paul's Cathedral. They attended theater performances in the West End, losing themselves in the stories that unfolded on stage, and spent countless hours in small, tucked-away cafés, discussing their favorite books and authors over steaming cups of tea.

One particularly memorable evening, Edward took Li Wei to the Royal Opera House. It was her first time attending an opera, and the experience left her spellbound. The grandeur of the venue, with its ornate chandeliers and velvet seats, took her breath away. As the orchestra began to play and the performers' voices soared through the air, Li Wei felt herself being transported to another world, one filled with passion, tragedy, and beauty.

When the final notes faded and the curtain fell, Li Wei sat in stunned silence, her heart racing with the intensity of the emotions the performance had stirred within her. As they left the opera house, stepping out into the cool night air, she turned to Edward, her eyes shining with gratitude and wonder.

"Thank you for tonight, Edward," she said softly. "It was truly magical."

Edward smiled, his expression tender. "I'm glad you enjoyed it. I wanted to share something special with you, something that might help you see things in a new light."

As their relationship continued to blossom, the bond between them grew stronger with each passing day. But despite the joy she found in Edward's company, Li Wei's internal struggle remained unresolved. The conflicting loyalties between her duty to her family and her feelings for Edward pulled her in different directions, tearing at the fabric of her peace.

One rainy afternoon, as they sat in a cozy café near Edward's flat, the sound of raindrops tapping against the window like an endless symphony, Edward broached the subject that had been weighing on both their minds. The café was a small, intimate place, with dim lighting and the comforting aroma of freshly brewed coffee. They sat in a corner booth, the world outside reduced to a blur of gray as the rain poured down.

"Li Wei," Edward began, his voice soft yet firm, "have you thought about what you want to do? About your engagement and your future?"

Li Wei stared into her cup of tea, the steam rising in delicate tendrils, her thoughts a tangled web of fear, love, and obligation. "I think about it every day, Edward," she admitted, her voice heavy with the weight of her dilemma. "I know what my family expects of me, and I don't want to disappoint them. But... I also know how I feel about you. It's tearing me apart."

Edward reached across the table, taking her hand in his. His touch was warm, reassuring, a lifeline in the stormy sea of her emotions. "You have to follow your heart, Li Wei," he said gently. "I know it's not easy, but you deserve to be happy. Whatever you decide, I'll support you. Just know that you're not alone in this."

Li Wei squeezed his hand, a lump forming in her throat. She knew he was right, but the path forward seemed impossibly difficult. The thought of hurting Yufei, of disappointing her parents, filled her with dread. And yet, the idea of leaving Edward, of returning to a life that no longer felt like hers, was equally unbearable.

As the days turned into weeks, Li Wei's anxiety grew. Her emotions were a tumultuous sea, tossing her between the shores of duty and desire. She knew she needed to make a decision, but the stakes were high, and the consequences of her choice loomed large, casting a shadow over every moment of her day.

One evening, as she lay in bed, staring up at the ceiling, her phone buzzed with a message from Yufei. His messages had become a regular occurrence, each one a reminder of the life waiting for her back in China, a life that felt increasingly distant, like a dream she could no longer quite recall.

"How are you, Li Wei? I miss you and can't wait for you to come home," the message read, the words simple yet laced with emotion.

Li Wei's heart ached as she read his words. Yufei was a good man, kind and considerate, and she knew he cared for her deeply. But her feelings for Edward were undeniable, and the thought of leaving him behind filled her with a sense of loss so profound it was almost physical.

Desperate for guidance, Li Wei sought refuge in the words of her grandmother, who had always been a source of wisdom and comfort. She remembered her grandmother's voice, soft yet firm, as she shared stories of love and sacrifice, of following one's heart even when the path was difficult. But could she really go against her family's wishes? Could she risk it all for a chance at happiness?

As Li Wei struggled with her decision, the days in London began to blur together, a whirlwind of emotions and experiences that left her feeling both exhilarated and exhausted. The city, once a place of discovery and adventure, now seemed to close in around her, its narrow streets and towering buildings reflecting the claustrophobia she felt within her own heart.

Finally, one evening, as she and Edward walked along the South Bank, the river Thames flowing dark and steady beside them, Li Wei knew she couldn't delay the inevitable any longer. The sky was painted in shades of twilight, the city lights beginning to twinkle like stars in the gathering dusk. She stopped, turning to Edward, her heart pounding in her chest.

"Edward," she began, her voice trembling, "I can't keep living in this limbo. I have to make a decision, one way or the other."

Edward's expression was unreadable, his eyes searching hers for a moment before he nodded. "I understand, Li Wei. Whatever you decide, I'll respect it. Just know that I care about you deeply, and I want you to be happy."

Tears welled up in Li Wei's eyes as she looked at him, her heart breaking at the thought of what she might have to give up. She knew she couldn't please everyone, that someone was going to be hurt no matter what she chose. But as she stood there, with the city spread out before her, she realized that she had to be true to herself, whatever the cost.

The storm within her raged on, but in that moment, Li Wei found a sliver of clarity. She knew that the road ahead would be difficult, filled with challenges and heartache. But she also knew that she couldn't keep running from the truth.

As they continued their walk, the city around them alive with the sounds of the night, Li Wei made a silent vow to herself. Whatever decision she made, it would be one she could live with, one that would allow her to look back without regret.

The dilemma remained unresolved, but for the first time in weeks, Li Wei felt a sense of calm. She didn't have all the answers yet, but she was beginning to find the courage to seek them out. And as she walked beside Edward, the warmth of his presence reassuring her, she knew that whatever happened, she wouldn't have to face it alone.

Chapter 6: Revelations

Li Wei sat in her small London flat, the dim glow of the desk lamp casting long shadows on the walls. Books and notes were scattered around her, remnants of her tireless studying. Her mind, however, was far from her academic pursuits. Instead, it was entangled in the emotional labyrinth of her recent decisions.

She had made a choice to follow her heart and pursue a relationship with Edward, yet the consequences of that choice reverberated through every aspect of her life. Her family's expectations, Yufei's understanding yet saddened acceptance, and the burgeoning love she felt for Edward created a complex tapestry of emotions that she struggled to unravel.

As she stared out the window, the city lights of London twinkling in the distance, her phone buzzed, breaking the silence. It was a message from her mother.

"Li Wei, we are proud of you and your choices. Remember, we always support you. Love, Mama."

Her mother's words brought a tear to her eye. The unconditional support from her family was a lifeline in these turbulent times. She took a deep breath, letting the comfort of her mother's message settle over her like a warm blanket.

The next day, Li Wei had an important lecture on Victorian literature. She dressed carefully, trying to shake off the emotional fog that had settled over her. As she walked to the lecture hall, she replayed her conversations with Yufei and her mother in her mind, their voices mingling with her thoughts.

Professor Matthews, an elderly man with a passion for literature, began the lecture with a quote from Charles Dickens. Li Wei tried to focus, but her mind kept drifting to Edward. She remembered the way his eyes lit up when he talked about his favorite books, the way his laughter filled the air with warmth.

After the lecture, Li Wei headed to the library, seeking solace in the familiar rows of books. She found a quiet corner and settled in with her notes. Yet, despite her best efforts, her thoughts kept returning to Edward.

That evening, Edward had invited her to dinner at his flat. He had promised to cook a special meal, a blend of British and Chinese cuisines. As she walked to his place, a mix of excitement and nervousness filled her. Their relationship had reached a new level of intimacy, and she was eager yet apprehensive about the future.

Edward greeted her with a warm smile and a hug. "I hope you're hungry," he said, leading her to the dining table. The table was set beautifully, with candles and flowers creating a romantic atmosphere. The aroma of the food made her stomach growl in anticipation.

As they ate, their conversation flowed effortlessly, touching on various topics from their favorite books to future dreams. Edward shared stories of his childhood, painting a vivid picture of his life before London.

"My parents have a small farm in the countryside," he said, his eyes filled with nostalgia. "I used to help with the animals and the garden. It was a simple life, but I loved it."

Li Wei listened, captivated by his stories. She shared her own memories of Guangzhou, the bustling city life, and her family's traditions.

"Guangzhou is a city of contrasts," she said. "Modern skyscrapers stand next to ancient temples. It's a place where tradition and modernity coexist."

Their conversation deepened, touching on more personal topics. Edward sensed her lingering sadness and gently broached the subject.

"Li Wei, I know it's been hard for you. How are you holding up with everything?"

She sighed, her emotions bubbling to the surface. "It's been difficult, Edward. I feel torn between my love for you and my duty to my family. Yufei has been understanding, but I know I've hurt him."

Edward reached across the table, taking her hand in his. "You've made a brave choice, Li Wei. It's not easy to follow your heart when it goes against tradition and expectations. But I believe we can find a way to make this work."

His words filled her with hope. They finished their meal, and Edward suggested they take a walk to clear their minds. The evening air was crisp and refreshing as they strolled through the nearby park.

As they walked, Edward shared more about his future plans. "I've been thinking about my career, Li Wei. I want to find a way to combine my love for literature with something more impactful. Maybe teaching or writing full-time."

Li Wei smiled, admiring his passion and determination. "You'd make a wonderful teacher, Edward. Your love for literature is contagious."

They continued walking, the conversation flowing easily between them. When they finally returned to Edward's flat, Li Wei felt a sense of peace she hadn't experienced in weeks.

Over the next few days, Li Wei found herself more focused and determined. Her relationship with Edward gave her strength, and her family's support provided a solid foundation. She threw herself into her studies, excelling in her classes and finding joy in her academic achievements.

Edward continued to be her anchor, his unwavering support and love a constant source of comfort. They spent their weekends exploring London, visiting museums, parks, and quaint cafes. Each experience brought them closer, deepening their connection.

One Saturday, Edward surprised her with a trip to the countryside. "I want to show you where I grew up," he said, his eyes sparkling with excitement.

They took a train to a small village surrounded by rolling hills and lush green fields. The air was fresh and filled with the scent of blooming flowers. Edward's parents welcomed them warmly, their home a cozy haven filled with love and warmth.

Edward's mother, a kind woman with a gentle smile, showed Li Wei around the garden. "Edward has told us so much about you," she said. "We're happy to finally meet you."

Li Wei felt a sense of belonging as she spent time with Edward's family. They shared stories, laughter, and delicious meals. The simplicity and tranquility of the countryside were a stark contrast to the hustle and bustle of London, and Li Wei found herself feeling rejuvenated.

As they walked through the fields one afternoon, Edward turned to Li Wei, his expression serious yet tender. "Li Wei, I know we have a long journey ahead, but I want you to know that I'm committed to us. I want to build a future with you."

Tears welled up in Li Wei's eyes as she took his hands in hers. "I want that too, Edward. I'm ready to face whatever challenges come our way, as long as we're together."

Their bond continued to strengthen, each day bringing new experiences and deeper understanding. Li Wei found herself growing more confident and self-assured. She knew the path ahead wouldn't be easy, but she was ready to embrace it with Edward by her side.

One evening, as they sat in a cozy café, Edward brought up the idea of visiting China together. "I'd love to see Guangzhou and meet your family," he said, his eyes filled with enthusiasm.

Li Wei's heart swelled with emotion. "I'd love that too, Edward. It would mean a lot to me."

As they made plans for their trip, Li Wei felt a sense of excitement and anticipation. She knew it would be a significant step in their relationship, bridging the gap between their cultures and families.

The weeks leading up to their trip were filled with preparations. Li Wei helped Edward learn basic Mandarin phrases, and they researched places to visit in Guangzhou. The anticipation of the trip brought a renewed sense of purpose and joy to their lives.

When the day finally arrived, Li Wei and Edward boarded the plane to Guangzhou, their hearts filled with hope and excitement. The journey was long, but they spent the time talking, laughing, and planning their adventures.

As the plane descended into Guangzhou, Li Wei felt a mix of emotions. She was eager to introduce Edward to her family and her city, yet nervous about their reactions. She took a deep breath, reminding herself of her mother's words of support.

At the airport, her parents greeted them with open arms. Edward's respectful demeanor and genuine interest in their culture quickly won them over. Her father, a man of few words, nodded approvingly as Edward attempted to speak Mandarin, his efforts met with smiles and encouragement.

Over the next few days, Li Wei showed Edward around Guangzhou, sharing her favorite spots and introducing him to the rich tapestry of her culture. They visited ancient temples, bustling markets, and serene gardens. Edward was captivated by the city's vibrancy and history, his admiration for Li Wei growing with each new experience.

One evening, as they sat with her family for dinner, Li Wei felt a profound sense of gratitude. Her two worlds had collided, and the result was a harmonious blend of love, understanding, and acceptance. She watched as Edward conversed with her parents, their laughter filling the room with warmth.

As the trip drew to a close, Li Wei knew they had taken a significant step forward. Their relationship had been tested and strengthened, their bond unbreakable. She felt a sense of peace and contentment, knowing that she had made the right choice.

Back in London, Li Wei and Edward continued to build their life together. They faced challenges with resilience and celebrated victories with joy. Their love was a beacon of hope, guiding them through the complexities of life.

Li Wei's journey had been filled with twists and turns, but she had emerged stronger and more self-assured. She had learned the importance of following her heart and embracing the unknown. With Edward by her side, she was ready to face whatever the future held.

Their story was one of love, courage, and the beauty of embracing life's uncertainties. Together, they forged a path filled with promise and endless possibilities, their hearts intertwined in a dance of love and hope.of her family's expectations pressing down on her. Yet, with Edward's support, she began to see the possibility of a future where she could be true to herself.

The journey ahead was uncertain, but Li Wei knew she wasn't alone. Edward was by her side, offering his unwavering support as she navigated the complexities of her heart and her future. And for the first time, Li Wei allowed herself to dream of a life where she could embrace both love and freedom.

Chapter 7: A Test of Love

As the weeks turned into months, Li Wei and Edward's relationship blossomed. The transition from the initial excitement of newfound love to the deeper, enduring connection of a committed relationship was both exhilarating and challenging. They faced numerous trials, each one testing the strength of their bond.

It was a sunny Saturday morning when Edward received a phone call that would change the course of their lives. He was lounging on the couch, reading a book, while Li Wei prepared breakfast in the kitchen. The sound of the ringing phone broke the peaceful silence.

"Hello?" Edward answered, his voice curious.

"Edward, it's your father. I have some news," came the voice from the other end, tinged with concern. "Your mother's health has taken a turn for the worse. The doctors say it's serious."

Edward's heart sank. His mother had been battling an illness for some time, but they had hoped she was on the mend. The gravity of his father's words hit him hard.

"I'll come home right away," Edward replied, his voice steady despite the turmoil inside.

After hanging up, he turned to Li Wei, who had been watching him with concern. "My mother's not doing well. I need to go back to the countryside to be with her."

Li Wei immediately moved to his side, wrapping her arms around him in a comforting embrace. "I'll come with you, Edward. You shouldn't go through this alone."

Edward's eyes softened as he looked at her. "Thank you, Li Wei. Your support means everything to me."

They quickly packed their bags and made arrangements to leave for the countryside. The train ride was long and somber, filled with an unspoken tension. Li Wei held Edward's hand, offering silent support as he gazed out the window, lost in thought.

Upon arriving at Edward's family home, they were greeted by his father, whose weary expression spoke volumes. He embraced Edward tightly, then turned to Li Wei with a grateful smile.

"Thank you for coming, Li Wei. Your presence is a great comfort to us," Edward's father said.

Inside the house, the atmosphere was heavy with concern. Edward's mother lay in bed, her frail body a stark contrast to the vibrant woman Li Wei had met months earlier. She smiled weakly as Edward and Li Wei entered the room.

"Edward, my boy," she whispered, her voice barely audible. "And Li Wei, it's so good to see you both."

Edward knelt beside her, taking her hand gently. "We're here, Mum. We're going to take care of you."

Li Wei watched with a heavy heart as Edward's mother struggled to speak, her words filled with love and gratitude. The days that followed were a blur of doctors' visits, medication schedules, and sleepless nights. Edward and Li Wei worked together, supporting each other through the emotional strain.

In the quiet moments, Li Wei would sit by the window, reflecting on the journey that had brought them to this point. She admired Edward's strength and devotion, his unwavering commitment to his family. It deepened her love for him, reinforcing her decision to stand by his side.

One evening, as they sat in the garden, Edward turned to Li Wei, his eyes filled with gratitude. "I couldn't have gotten through this without you, Li Wei. You've been my rock."

Li Wei smiled softly, reaching out to hold his hand. "We're in this together, Edward. Your family is my family now."

Edward's mother's condition fluctuated, with moments of hope followed by periods of despair. Li Wei became an integral part of the family's support system, her presence a source of comfort and stability.

One particularly difficult night, Edward's mother experienced a severe setback. The family gathered around her bedside, their faces etched with worry. Li Wei held Edward's hand tightly, praying for a miracle.

As dawn broke, the doctor arrived with a somber expression. He delivered the news they had been dreading: Edward's mother's condition was critical, and there was little more they could do.

Edward's father broke down in tears, and Edward held him close, his own eyes brimming with sorrow. Li Wei stood by, her heart aching for the family she had come to love.

In the days that followed, they made the difficult decision to bring Edward's mother home for her final days. They wanted her to be surrounded by the love and warmth of her family.

Li Wei took on the role of caretaker, helping with the daily tasks and providing emotional support. She and Edward shared quiet moments, finding solace in each other's company. The bond between them grew stronger, forged in the crucible of shared pain and resilience.

One afternoon, as Li Wei sat by Edward's mother's bedside, the older woman reached out and took her hand. Her eyes, though weak, held a spark of clarity.

"Li Wei, thank you for being here," she said softly. "You've brought so much light into our lives. Take care of my Edward. He's a good man."

Tears welled up in Li Wei's eyes as she nodded, her heart heavy with emotion. "I promise I will."

In the quiet moments that followed, Edward's mother closed her eyes, a peaceful expression settling over her face. She passed away surrounded by love, her family holding her close.

The funeral was a solemn affair, attended by family and friends from the village. Edward delivered a heartfelt eulogy, his voice steady despite the tears in his eyes. Li Wei stood by his side, offering silent strength.

After the funeral, they returned to London, their hearts heavy with grief. The experience had changed them, deepening their love and commitment to each other. They found solace in their shared memories, drawing strength from the bond they had forged.

In the weeks that followed, Edward focused on his studies and his plans for the future. Li Wei supported him, offering encouragement and love. They spent quiet evenings together, finding comfort in each other's presence.

One evening, as they sat on the couch, Edward turned to Li Wei, his eyes filled with determination. "I want to write a book about our journey, Li Wei. About the challenges we've faced and the love that's carried us through."

Li Wei smiled, her heart swelling with pride. "I think that's a wonderful idea, Edward. Your story deserves to be told."

Edward began working on his book, pouring his heart and soul into the pages. Li Wei watched as he wrote, admiring his passion and dedication. She knew their love was a source of inspiration, a beacon of hope in the face of adversity.

As the months passed, Edward's book took shape, each chapter a testament to their journey. He dedicated the book to his mother, whose love and strength had been a guiding light in his life.

When the book was finally published, it received widespread acclaim. Readers were moved by the story of love, resilience, and the unbreakable bond between two people from different worlds.

Li Wei and Edward continued to build their life together, facing each new challenge with courage and determination. Their love was a source of strength, a reminder that they could overcome anything as long as they had each other.

Their journey was far from over, but they faced the future with hope and optimism. Together, they had weathered the storms of life and emerged stronger, their love a testament to the power of the human spirit.

As they looked back on their journey, they knew that the road ahead would be filled with both joy and sorrow. But they were ready to face it together, their hearts intertwined in a dance of love and hope.

And so, their story continued a beautiful tapestry of love, resilience, and the enduring power of the human spirit. They faced each new day with courage and determination, knowing their love would carry them through whatever challenges.

Chapter 8: The Letters from Home

The crisp air of early autumn whispered through the streets of London, carrying with it the scent of fallen leaves and distant memories. Li Wei sat by the window of her small but cozy apartment, gazing out at the world below. The city was alive with its usual bustle, but today, she felt a sense of detachment from it all. Her thoughts were elsewhere, a thousand miles away, in a place she had left behind but never truly forgotten.

It was a quiet morning when the letters arrived. Li Wei had been going about her usual routine, preparing a simple breakfast of tea and toast, when the soft thud of the mail hitting the floor caught her attention. She had grown accustomed to the mundane deliveries bills, advertisements, and the occasional postcard from a friend. But today, as she sifted through the stack, her breath caught in her throat.

There, among the ordinary envelopes, were two letters that stood out like relics from another time. The first was from her mother, the familiar handwriting instantly recognizable, the strokes gentle yet firm. The second was from her younger brother, his script more hurried and uneven, a reflection of his youthful energy. The sight of these letters, so unexpected, sent a rush of emotions through Li Wei surprise, nostalgia, and a pang of homesickness that she had buried deep within her heart.

She hesitated for a moment, the letters trembling slightly in her hands. It had been months since she had last spoken to her family, the distance between them not just physical but emotional as well. Her decision to leave China and pursue her studies in London had been met with resistance, particularly from her father. Though her mother had been more understanding, the rift it had created in their family had left wounds that had yet to heal.

Li Wei moved to the couch, the letters resting on her lap as she took a deep breath. The apartment was quiet, save for the distant hum of traffic outside. She picked up her mother's letter first, running her fingers over the delicate paper before carefully opening it. The familiar scent of her mother's perfume wafted up, bringing with it a flood of memories afternoons spent in the kitchen, the sound of her mother's laughter, the warmth of her embrace.

"Dear Li Wei," the letter began, and as she read, her mother's voice seemed to echo in her mind, soft and soothing.

Her mother wrote about life back home, how the seasons had changed, and how the garden Li Wei had once tended was now in full bloom. She spoke of the neighbors, the small-town gossip, and the family's daily routines. But beneath the surface of these mundane details, Li Wei could sense the unspoken words, the longing, and the quiet worry that only a mother could feel.

"I miss you, my dear," the letter continued. "Your father and I think of you every day. We hope that you are well, that you are finding happiness in your studies and in your new life. But I must admit, the house feels emptier without you here. Your father doesn't say it, but I know he misses you too, in his own way."

Li Wei felt tears prick at the corners of her eyes. She had always been close to her mother, and reading her words now, so full of love and tenderness, brought back the ache of being so far from home. Her mother went on to mention her father's health, how he had been working too hard, and how she worried about him.

"Please write to us when you can," her mother concluded. "We want to know how you are, truly. Take care of yourself, Li Wei. We love you more than words can say."

Li Wei set the letter down, wiping away a tear that had escaped. The weight of her mother's love and concern pressed heavily on her heart. She had chosen this path, to leave everything behind and start anew in London, but the cost of that choice was becoming clearer with each passing day.

Taking a deep breath, she reached for the second letter. Her brother's handwriting was more erratic, the ink smudged in places, as if he had written it in haste. She smiled as she opened it, already imagining his lively voice in her head.

"Hey sis," the letter began, and she could almost hear the mischievous grin in his tone. "It's been ages since you left, and things are so boring without you here to boss me around."

Her brother wrote about his school, his friends, and the latest antics that had gotten him into trouble. He complained about their father's strictness, about how he missed their late-night conversations, and how the house wasn't the same without her. But as the letter went on, his words took on a more serious tone.

"Li Wei, I know things were tough when you left. I didn't understand it at first, why you had to go so far away. But now, I think I get it. You needed to find your own way, and I'm proud of you for that. I just... I miss you, you know? And I worry about you being all alone over there."

Li Wei felt a lump form in her throat as she read his words. Her brother had always been the one to bring lightness to their home, his energy infectious and his spirit unbreakable. Knowing that he worried about her, that he missed her, made the distance between them feel even greater.

"Take care of yourself, okay?" the letter ended. "And don't forget about us. Come home when you can. We need you here."

As Li Wei folded the letter and placed it beside her mother's, she felt a deep sense of longing, a pull towards the home she had left behind. The letters had stirred something within her, a reminder of the life she had once known, the people who had shaped her, and the love that still bound them together, even across oceans.

For a long time, she sat there, the letters in her lap, her thoughts swirling like the autumn leaves outside. She had come to London to forge her own path, to escape the expectations that had weighed her down, but in doing so, she had also left behind a part of herself. The letters were a bridge, connecting her past to her present, reminding her that no matter how far she traveled, she could never truly leave her roots behind.

As the day slowly turned to dusk, Li Wei knew that she had to respond. She would write back to her family, to her mother and brother, and perhaps even to her father. She would share with them the life she was building in London, the challenges she faced, and the happiness she had found. But she would also let them know that she missed them, that she carried their love with her every day, and that she had not forgotten where she came from.

With renewed resolve, Li Wei rose from the couch and moved to her desk. She pulled out a sheet of paper, her pen poised above it. The words came slowly at first, but as she wrote, the dam broke, and the emotions she had been holding back poured out onto the page. She wrote with honesty, with love, and with a sense of peace that she had not felt in a long time.

By the time she finished, the room was bathed in the soft glow of the setting sun. Li Wei looked down at the letter she had written, feeling a sense of closure, a quiet acceptance of the past and the present. She knew that the road ahead would not be easy, but with her family's love and support, she felt ready to face whatever challenges lay ahead.

She carefully folded the letter and placed it in an envelope, sealing it with a sense of finality. As she prepared to send it off, she glanced out the window, watching as the last rays of sunlight dipped below the horizon. In that moment, Li Wei knew that she was not alone. She was connected to her family, to her roots, and to the world she was creating for herself in London.

And with that knowledge, she felt a renewed sense of purpose, ready to continue her journey, wherever it might lead.

Chapter 9: The Unexpected Reunion

Months had passed since Li Wei and Edward returned to London after the sorrowful loss of Edward's mother. The city, with its ever-changing hues and bustling energy, had begun to feel like home again, but beneath the surface of their day-to-day lives, the shadow of grief still lingered. They had learned to navigate their sorrow together, turning to each other for solace and finding in their shared pain a deepened bond that neither had anticipated.

As the autumn air grew crisp and the leaves turned to shades of gold and crimson, Li Wei slipped back into the routines she had known before their world had been upended. She threw herself into her studies with renewed vigor, and Edward immersed himself in his work, though their evenings were often spent in quiet companionship, the silence between them comforting rather than oppressive.

One such evening, as the golden light of dusk filtered through their apartment windows, Li Wei's phone chimed, signaling a new email. She glanced at it absently, expecting it to be something mundane. But as she read the sender's name her father's her heart skipped a beat. It had been so long since she had heard from him, and their last conversation had been fraught with tension and unspoken disappointment. With a mixture of trepidation and curiosity, she opened the message.

Her father's email was as brief and formal as she remembered, his words precise and to the point. He informed her that he would be traveling to London on a business trip the following week and expressed a desire to meet with her. Though the tone was distant, Li Wei detected an undercurrent of something she couldn't quite place. Was it a concern? Regret? Or merely the sense of duty that had always characterized their relationship?

Li Wei set her phone down, her mind swirling with conflicting emotions. She had left China with the intention of carving out a life of her own, a life her father had never truly understood or supported. The news of his impending visit filled her with a strange combination of excitement and dread. Would he still see her as the rebellious daughter who had defied his wishes, or would he recognize the person she had become a woman shaped by her own choices, for better or worse?

That evening, Li Wei and Edward ventured out to their favorite little bistro, a quaint, tucked-away gem with flickering candles on every table and the rich aroma of simmering sauces wafting through the air. The familiar setting usually brought her comfort, but tonight, her thoughts were too tangled to enjoy the ambiance.

As they sat down, Edward noticed her unease immediately. "You seem quiet tonight," he remarked, his eyes filled with concern as he reached across the table to take her hand.

Li Wei hesitated for a moment, gathering her thoughts before speaking. "I received an email from my father today," she began, her voice steady despite the turmoil inside her. "He's coming to London next week, and he wants to meet me."

Edward's brow furrowed slightly as he absorbed her words. "How do you feel about that?" he asked gently, his thumb tracing soothing circles on the back of her hand.

"I... I'm not sure," Li Wei admitted, her gaze dropping to the table. "We haven't seen each other since I left China, and our relationship has always been... complicated. He never approved of my decision to study abroad, let alone my choice to stay here and break off my engagement."

Edward listened intently, his expression thoughtful. "It sounds like this could be an important opportunity for both of you," he said after a moment. "To clear the air, maybe even to start rebuilding your relationship."

Li Wei nodded slowly, though her mind was still a jumble of what-ifs. "I'm just worried about how it will go. He's always been so critical of my choices. I'm not sure if anything has changed."

Edward squeezed her hand reassuringly. "Whatever happens, you won't have to face it alone," he said, his voice firm with resolve. "I'll be there with you, every step of the way."

Li Wei looked up at him, her heart swelling with gratitude. "Thank you, Edward," she whispered, her eyes glistening with unshed tears. "I don't know what I'd do without you."

The days leading up to her father's arrival were a whirlwind of anticipation and anxiety. Li Wei found herself constantly rehearsing potential conversations in her head, trying to anticipate her father's questions and criticisms. She spent hours preparing both physically and mentally, choosing her words with care and practicing how she would introduce Edward. All the while, Edward remained her steadfast anchor, offering quiet support and gentle encouragement whenever her nerves threatened to overwhelm her.

When the day finally arrived, Li Wei and Edward made their way to Heathrow Airport, the vast terminal bustling with travelers from all corners of the world. The cacophony of announcements, the hurried footsteps, and the hum of distant conversations created a dizzying backdrop as Li Wei stood at the arrival gate, her heart pounding in her chest.

She scanned the sea of faces, her eyes flitting from one traveler to the next until, at last, she spotted him. Her father emerged from the crowd, his posture as straight and imposing as ever, through the years had etched new lines into his once-unblemished face. His hair, now more silver than black, caught the fluorescent lights, and his eyes sharp and discerning seemed to take in everything around him with a single glance.

Li Wei's breath caught in her throat as she stepped forward, her voice trembling as she greeted him in Mandarin. "Father," she said, bowing slightly in a gesture of respect that felt both familiar and foreign after all this time.

Her father's gaze softened ever so slightly as he took her in, though his expression remained guarded. "Li Wei," he replied, his tone neutral. "It's good to see you."

Li Wei nodded, swallowing the lump in her throat. "This is Edward," she said, switching to English as she gestured toward the man at her side. "My... my boyfriend."

Edward extended his hand with a polite smile, his demeanor calm and confident despite the tension in the air. "It's a pleasure to meet you, sir," he said, his voice steady.

Her father regarded Edward with an inscrutable expression, his eyes narrowing slightly as he took in the young man before him. After a moment, he accepted the handshake, his grip firm but not overly so. "Nice to meet you, Edward," he said, though his tone was more measured than warm.

The car ride back to their apartment was filled with polite conversation, though the underlying tension was palpable. Li Wei's father asked about her studies, her life in London, and her plans for the future, his questions pointed and precise. He was civil to Edward, but Li Wei could sense the subtle undercurrents of disapproval in his tone, the unspoken judgments that had always characterized their relationship.

When they finally arrived at the apartment, Li Wei felt a wave of relief wash over her, though the tension still lingered in the air. Her father stepped inside, his eyes sweeping over the space with a critical eye. The apartment, though modest, was a reflection of both her and Edward—warm, inviting, and filled with personal touches that spoke to their shared life together.

"You have a nice place," her father commented after a moment, though his tone suggested he found it lacking in some indefinable way.

"Thank you, Father," Li Wei replied, her voice carefully measured as she forced a smile. "We've worked hard to make it feel like home."

There was a brief, awkward silence before her father spoke again, his gaze now fixed on her. "Li Wei," he began, his voice carrying a note of reproach. "Why didn't you tell me about Edward sooner?"

Li Wei's heart skipped a beat as she met her father's stern gaze. This was the conversation she had been dreading, the confrontation she had tried to prepare for but knew she could never fully anticipate. Taking a deep breath, she steadied herself before responding. "I didn't know how to, Father," she said, her voice quiet but firm. "I knew you wouldn't approve, and I didn't want to cause more tension between us."

Her father sighed, a sound filled with the weight of unspoken disappointment. "Li Wei, you are my only daughter," he said, his voice softening slightly. "I want what's best for you. But I have to admit, I was disappointed when you broke off your engagement and decided to stay in London."

Li Wei felt a pang of guilt, but she knew she had to stand her ground. "I understand that, Father," she replied, her voice steady. "But I had to follow my own path. Edward has been my support through everything. He's kind, intelligent, and he loves me."

Her father turned his gaze to Edward, who had been listening quietly, his expression respectful yet resolute. "Edward," her father said, his tone heavy with meaning, "I hope you understand the responsibilities and challenges that come with loving my daughter. She's precious to me."

Edward met his gaze without flinching, his expression earnest and sincere. "I understand, sir," he said, his voice filled with quiet conviction. "Li Wei means the world to me. I promise to support her, respect her, and love her with all my heart."

There was a long pause as her father considered Edward's words, the silence stretching out like a taut wire between them. Finally, after what felt like an eternity, her father nodded, though the gesture was slow and reluctant. "I can see that you care for her," he said, his voice measured. "That is important. But remember, actions speak louder than words."

The rest of the evening unfolded in a series of cautious conversations, the initial tension easing slightly as they moved on to more neutral topics. Li Wei's father shared stories of his

business endeavors, his tone more animated as he discussed familiar territory. Edward listened attentively, asking insightful questions that seemed to earn him a grudging respect from the older man.

As the night drew to a close and her father prepared to leave, Li Wei felt a strange mix of emotions—relief, exhaustion, and a glimmer of hope. The evening had not been easy, but it had not been the disaster she had feared either. There were still many bridges to build, many wounds to heal, but for the first time in a long while, she felt that perhaps, just perhaps, they could find a way forward.

Her father paused at the door, turning to her with an unreadable expression. "Li Wei," he said, his voice softer than she had ever heard it. "I am proud of the woman you've become, even if I don't always agree with your choices."

Li Wei felt a lump form in her throat as she met her father's gaze. "Thank you, Father," she whispered, her voice thick with emotion. "That means a lot to me."

With a final nod, her father stepped out into the cool night air, the door closing softly behind him. Li Wei stood there for a moment, staring at the closed door, her heart pounding in her chest. Then she turned to Edward, who was watching her with a warm, supportive smile.

"You did great," he said, pulling her into a gentle embrace. "He's a tough man, but I think you made an impression on him."

Li Wei leaned into his embrace, feeling the tension slowly melt away. "I couldn't have done it without you," she murmured, her voice filled with gratitude.

As they stood there in the quiet of their apartment, Li Wei felt a sense of peace settle over her, a feeling that perhaps, despite the challenges ahead, everything would be okay. For the first time in a long while, she felt that she was exactly where she was meant to be between two worlds, but no longer alone.